# ¡Felicidades!
# Congratulations!

*para*
*to* ...................................................................

*de*
*from* ...................................................................

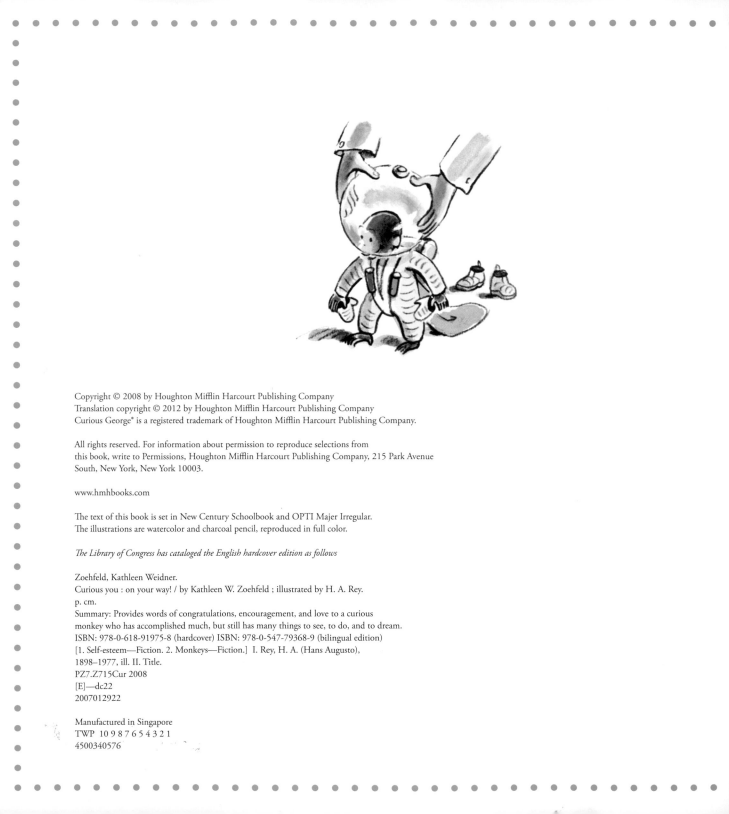

www.hmhbooks.com

The text of this book is set in New Century Schoolbook and OPTI Majer Irregular.
The illustrations are watercolor and charcoal pencil, reproduced in full color.

*The Library of Congress has cataloged the English hardcover edition as follows*

Zoehfeld, Kathleen Weidner.
Curious you : on your way! / by Kathleen W. Zoehfeld ; illustrated by H. A. Rey.
p. cm.
Summary: Provides words of congratulations, encouragement, and love to a curious
monkey who has accomplished much, but still has many things to see, to do, and to dream.
ISBN: 978-0-618-91975-8 (hardcover) ISBN: 978-0-547-79368-9 (bilingual edition)
[1. Self-esteem—Fiction. 2. Monkeys—Fiction.]  I. Rey, H. A. (Hans Augusto),
1898–1977, ill. II. Title.
PZ7.Z715Cur 2008
[E]—dc22
2007012922

Manufactured in Singapore
TWP  10 9 8 7 6 5 4 3 2 1
4500340576

# ¡Eres curioso todo el tiempo!
# Curious You On Your Way!

Escrito por / Written by  Kathleen W. Zoehfeld

Ilustrado por / Illustrated by  H. A. Rey

Traducido por / Translated by  Carlos E. Calvo

HOUGHTON MIFFLIN HARCOURT

BOSTON   NEW YORK   2012

**¡HIP, HIP, HURRA!**
Has hecho cosas geniales.

# HIP, HIP, HOORAY!

You've done great things.

Todo el mundo está orgulloso de **TI**.

The whole world is proud of **YOU** today.

Aprendiste mucho.
Estudiaste mucho.

You've learned so much.
You studied hard.

Y pusiste tu cabeza a pensar.
And put your brains to the test.

¡Jugaste en el equipo!

You played on the team!

Pero claro, llega un momento en que un monito curioso **¡debe salir!**
Of course, the time comes when a curious monkey needs to **break free!**

Aunque no sepas exactamente adónde vas . . .
Even if it means you don't know exactly where you're going . . .

ni qué pasará.
or what will come next.

¡Hay mucho para **ver**!
So much to **see!**

¡Hay mucho para **probar**!
So much to **try!**

¿Qué debes **hacer**?
What should you **do?**

Depende de **TI.**

It's up to **YOU.**

Simplemente sigue tus sueños y déjate llevar.
Just follow your dreams and you'll soar.

A veces te puede dar un poco de
miedo. Pero . . . ¡agárrate fuerte!
You may feel a little frightened
at times. But . . . hold on tight!

¡Tendrás una vista panorámica que te dejará sin aliento!
You'll see sights that take your breath away!

Encontrarás lugares ideales para aterrizar.

**Y**ou'll find the spot where you most want to land.

¡Oh! ¡Qué lugares increíbles!

## Oh, what a place it will be!

Sentirás la emoción de descubrir cosas.
The thrill of discovery will be yours.

Y si todo no sale como lo planeas . . . **¡no te preocupes!**
And if things don't work out quite as you had planned . . .

# don't worry!

Todos los exploradores **tropiezan** y **chocan** algunas veces.

All great explorers **bump** and **crash** sometimes.

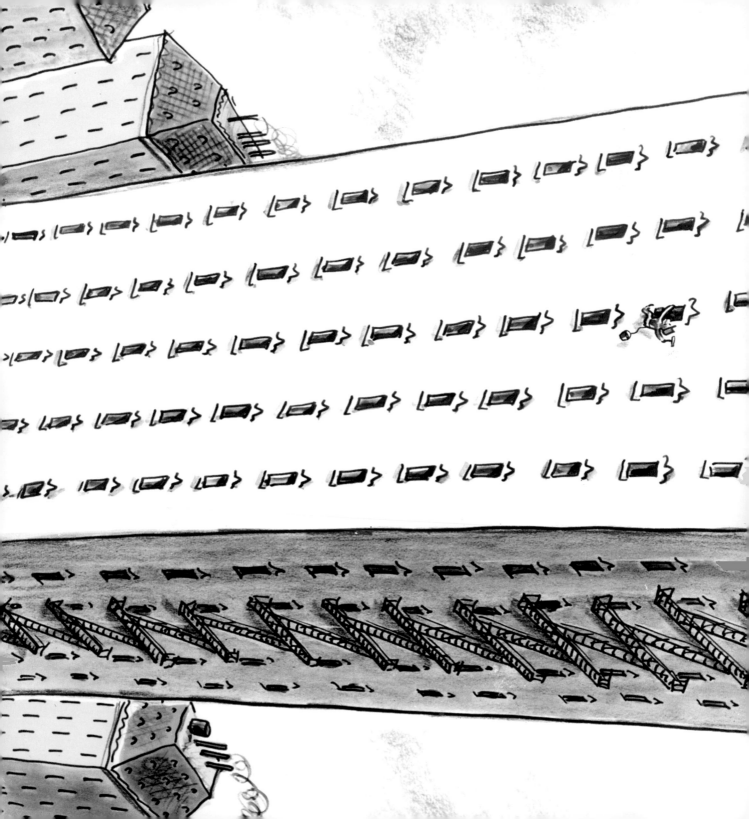

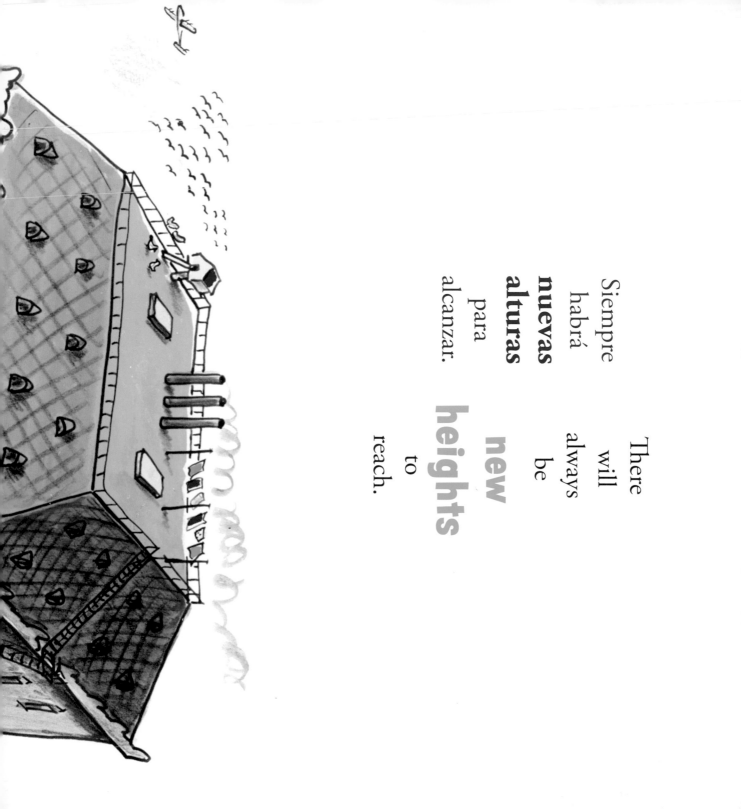

Siempre
habrá
**nuevas**
**alturas**
para
alcanzar.

There
will
always
be
**new**
**heights**
to
reach.

Cualquier cosa que hagas,
**tendrá tu estilo**.
Whatever you do, you will
**find your own style.**

¡Aunque eso **sorprenda** a algunas personas!
Even if it **surprises** a few!

Harás cosas por otros
como sólo tú sabes hacerlas.
You'll give to others in
ways that only you can.

Y harás nuevos amigos.
And you will make new friends.

El mundo te necesita.
The world needs you now.

Tú tienes **GRANDES** ideas.

You've got

**BIG**

ideas.

Debes intentar todas las hazañas que te imagines . . .
y la imaginación te llevará a la invención.
The feats you imagine you'll just have to try . . .
and imagination can lead to invention.

Antes de que te des cuenta
Before you know it,

**TODOS LOS OJOS** estarán puestos en **TI**.

the **SPOTLIGHT** will be on **YOU**.

**¿Cuál será tu historia?**
Audaz e inspiradora,
¡una historia de curiosidad y de valiente exploración!
¡Todos harán fila para ver!

# What will your story be?

Bold and inspiring—
a tale of curiosity
and brave exploration!
Everyone will line up to see!

Y si en el camino que eliges hay tropiezos . . .
And if the path that you choose gets rocky and rough—

Si en algún momento te sientes solo . . .
whenever you feel all alone—

recuerda, estaremos contigo todo el tiempo. Hoy, mañana . . .
remember, we're with you all the way. Today, tomorrow . . .

¡y todos los días!
and every day!

Estamos orgullosos de que **TÚ** seas tan **curioso**.

We're proud of **curious YOU.**